I AM
LOVED

To Kwame, my wonderful, positive friend
—N. G.

To Ginney
—A. B.

ATHENEUM BOOKS FOR YOUNG READERS
An imprint of Simon & Schuster Children's Publishing Division
1230 Avenue of the Americas, New York, New York 10020
"Kidnap Poem" from *Black Feeling, Black Talk, Black Judgment* by Nikki Giovanni.
Copyright © 1970 by Nikki Giovanni. Courtesy of HarperCollins Publishers.
"Paula the Cat" from *Vacation Time* by Nikki Giovanni. Copyright © 1980 by
Nikki Giovanni. Courtesy of HarperCollins Publishers.
"Quilts" from *Acolytes* by Nikki Giovanni. Copyright © 2007 by
Nikki Giovanni. Courtesy of HarperCollins Publishers.
"No Heaven" from *Bicycles* by Nikki Giovanni. Copyright © 2009 by
Nikki Giovanni. Courtesy of HarperCollins Publishers.
All other text copyright © 2018 by Nikki Giovanni
Illustrations copyright © 2018 by The Ashley Bryan Center, a Maine Corporation
All rights reserved, including the right of reproduction in whole or in part in any form.
ATHENEUM BOOKS FOR YOUNG READERS is a registered trademark of
Simon & Schuster, Inc. Atheneum logo is a trademark of Simon & Schuster, Inc.
For information about special discounts for bulk purchases, please contact
Simon & Schuster Special Sales at 1-866-506-1949 or business@simonandschuster.com.
The Simon & Schuster Speakers Bureau can bring authors to your live event.
For more information or to book an event, contact the Simon & Schuster
Speakers Bureau at 1-866-248-3049 or visit our website at www.simonspeakers.com.
Book design by Ann Bobco and Vikki Sheatsley
The text for this book was set in ITC Novarese.
The illustrations for this book were rendered in tempera and watercolor.
Manufactured in China • 0919 SCP
6 8 10 9 7 5
CIP data for this book is available from the Library of Congress.
ISBN 978-1-5344-0492-2 • ISBN 978-1-5344-0493-9 (eBook)

I AM LOVED

poems by
Nikki Giovanni

illustrations by
Ashley Bryan

A Caitlyn Dlouhy Book

Atheneum Books for Young Readers

New York London Toronto Sydney New Delhi

Because

I wrote a poem
for you because
you are
my little boy

I wrote a poem
for you because
you are
my darling daughter

and in this poem
I sang a song
that says
as time goes on
I am you
and you are me
and that's how life
goes on

Leaves

On a rainy day
When I'm sitting
In a tree
Looking for a friend
I hope you'll be the one
Standing at the root
Holding out your arms
To gently catch
My fall

Wild Flowers

We are like a field . . . of wild flowers . . . unpollinated . . . swaying against the wind.

Dew sparkling . . . buds bursting . . . we await the drying day. . . . Let's not gain . . . the notice of the woman . . . with the large straw basket. . . .

Autumn will come . . . anyway. . . . Let us continue . . . our dance . . . beneath the sun. . . .

Quilts

(for Sally Sellers)

Like a fading piece of cloth
I am a failure.

No longer do I cover tables filled with food and laughter.
My seams are frayed my hems falling
My strength no longer able
To hold the hot and cold.

I wish for those first days
When just woven I could keep water
From seeping through
Repel stains with the tightness of my weave
Dazzle the sunlight with my
Reflection.

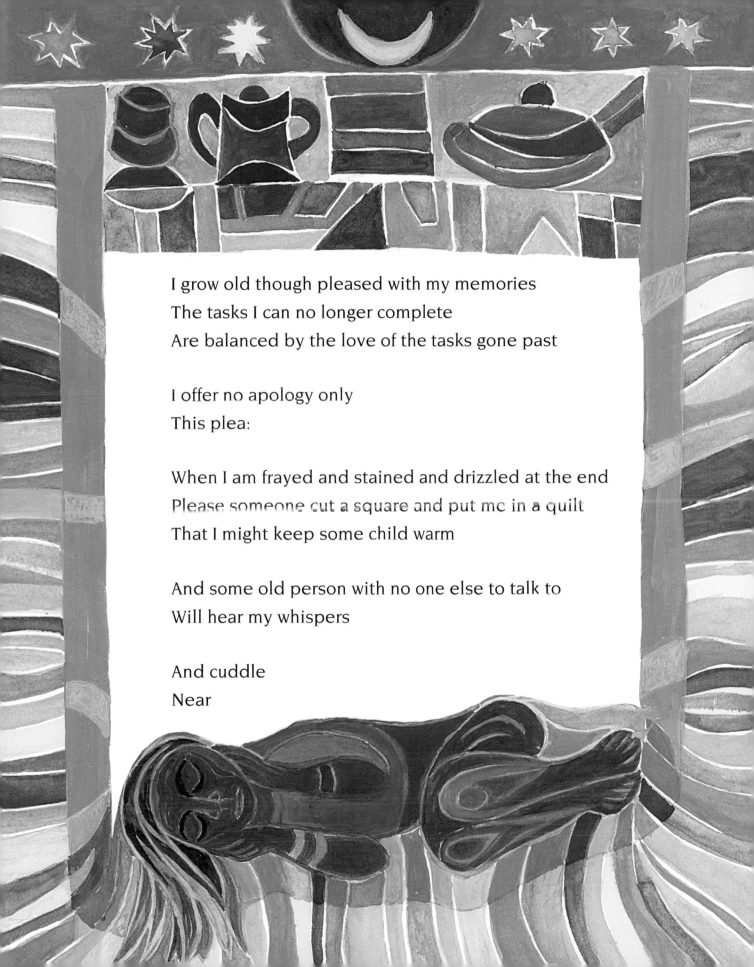

I grow old though pleased with my memories
The tasks I can no longer complete
Are balanced by the love of the tasks gone past

I offer no apology only
This plea:

When I am frayed and stained and drizzled at the end
Please someone cut a square and put me in a quilt
That I might keep some child warm

And some old person with no one else to talk to
Will hear my whispers

And cuddle
Near

A Song of a Blackbird

(for Carolyn Rodgers, October 4, 2010)

We look for words:
    intelligent   intense
    chocolate   warm
    ambitious   cautious

to describe a person

We design monuments:
    the Pyramids   the Taj Mahal
    the Lincoln Memorial   the Empire State Building
    the Wrigley Building   Coffins

to say someone was loved

We sing a sad blue
    Song
We sing a river—no—bridge
    Song
We sing a Song of a Blackbird
    To say

You will be missed.

Three/Quarters Time

Dance with me . . . dance with me . . . we are the song . . . we
are the music . . . Dance with me . . .
Waltz me . . . twirl me . . . do-si-do, please . . . peppermint twist
me . . . philly
squeeze

Cha-cha-cha . . . tango . . . two-step too . . .
Cakewalk . . . Charleston . . . boogaloo . . .

Dance with me . . . dance with me . . . All night long . . .
We are the music . . . we are the song . . .

Kidnap Poem

ever been kidnapped
by a poet
if i were a poet
i'd kidnap you
put you in my phrases and meter
you to jones beach
or maybe coney island
or maybe just to my house
lyric you in lilacs
dash you in the rain
blend into the beach
to complement my see
play the lyre for you
ode you with my love song
anything to win you
wrap you in the red Black green
show you off to mama
yeah if i were a poet i'd kid
nap you

Paula the Cat

Paula the cat
not thin nor fat
is as happy as house cats can be

She reads and she writes
with all the delights
of intelligent cats up a tree

Tired of the view
she chose to pursue
a fate unbeknownst to the crowd

Finding a boat
locked up in a moat
she boarded and shouted out loud

I'm Paula the cat
not thin nor fat
as happy as house cats can be

But now I've the urge
for my spirit to surge
and I shall go off
to sea

No Heaven

How can there be
No heaven

How can there be
No Heaven

When rain falls
gently on the grass
When sunshine scampers
across my toes

When tears comfort
When dreams caress
When you smile
 at me

When corn bakes
into bread
When wheat melts
into cake

When shadows
cool
And owls
call
And little finches
eat upside
down

I Am a Mirror

I am a mirror

I reflect the grace
Of my mother
The tenacity
Of my grandmother
The patience
Of my grandfather
The sweat
Of my great-grandmother
The hope
Of my great-grandfather
The songs
Of my ancestors
The prayers
Of those on the auction block
The bravery
Of those in the middle passage

I reflect the strengths
Of my people
And for that alone
I am loved

Do the Rosa Parks

(A Song in Rhythm)

do the rosa parks
say no no

do the rosa parks
throw your hands in the air

do the rosa parks
say . . . no no

do the rosa parks
tell them that's not fair

somebody's lying
rosa parks him
somebody's crying
rosa parks her

shame the bad
comfort the good
do the rosa parks
just like she would

sit down (1, 2, 3, 4, 5, 6)
stand up (1, 2, 3, 4, 5, 6)
sit down (1, 2, 3, 4, 5, 6)
do the rosa parks all over town

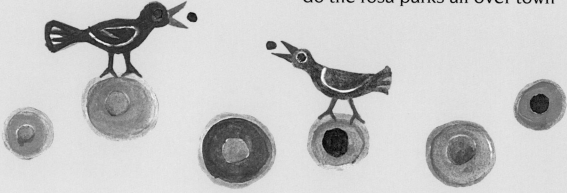

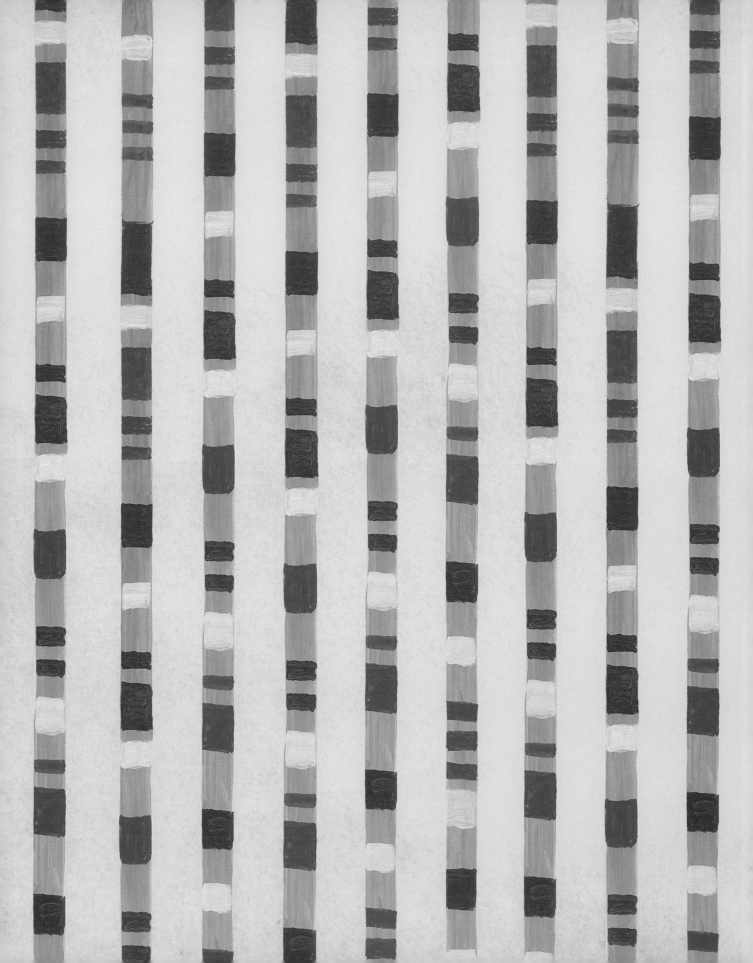